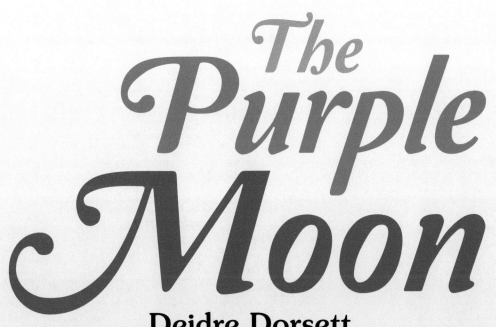

The Purple Moon

Deidre Dorsett

Balboa Press books may be ordered through booksellers or by contacting:

Balboa Press
A Division of Hay House
1663 Liberty Drive
Bloomington, IN 47403
www.balboapress.com
844-682-1282

Because of the dynamic nature of the Internet, any web addresses or links contained in this book may have changed since publication and may no longer be valid. The views expressed in this work are solely those of the author and do not necessarily reflect the views of the publisher, and the publisher hereby disclaims any responsibility for them.

Any people depicted in stock imagery provided by Getty Images are models, and such images are being used for illustrative purposes only.
Certain stock imagery © Getty Images.

Interior Image Credit: Deidre Dorsett

ISBN: 978-1-9822-6885-5 (sc)
978-1-9822-6886-2 (e)

Library of Congress Control Number: 2021909826

Print information available on the last page.

Balboa Press rev. date: 05/24/2021

BALBOA.PRESS
A DIVISION OF HAY HOUSE

Introduction

"But then there was beauty to be seen brightly shining when with the blessed choir, the souls beheld the beautific spectacle and vision and were perfected in that mystery of mysteries which it is to meet to call the most blessed. This did we celebrate in our true perfect selves, when we were yet untouched by all the evils in time to come; when as initiates we were allowed to see perfect and simple, still and happy. Purer was the light that shone around us, and pure were we."

– Socrates

I close my eyes and begin to pray; I thank the universe for this lovely day!

Who am I? Anyone you want me to be. Where am I? Look into thee and you'll see. I am simply we. I feel my spirit going free, a cool breeze soothes me. I touch my face it has escaped me, my hands where could they be? Through the window I go, the stars call me this I know.

What a wonderful place to be, I am truly free!

The wind whispers to me, you are free and you are WE!!

I am flying over water so crystal clear.
The smell of flowers so sweet and dear.

Higher and higher I go; my spirit feels so wonderful! I hear birds singing in harmony, because they know my spirit is free.

I DANCED WITH THE STARS!!

I fly straight into the stars; the beautiful blue sky consumes me. This feeling is very beautiful you see. I am a star; the stars are me; we shine together so bright and free. I dance with the stars; they dance with me. I am the sky now, the sky is me, the big beautiful sky tickles me. The universe is truly embracing me.

MY CURIOSITY GOT THE BEST OF ME!

I go even higher and higher; I look straight ahead way above me;
I see a PURPLE MOON!!

A beautiful purple the way you would imagine purple to be. Closer
and closer I go; my curiosity has the best of me. This purple moon
is for me, this I know. The purple moon is where my spirit must go.

As I get closer a strong wind puts out its hand.

I submerged deeper and deeper into this strange and wonderful purple land.

AS I GET CLOSER THE WIND STARTS TO BLOW

THE PURPLE MOON IS FOR ME THIS I KNOW!

Around and around, I went, I have a feeling of such grand content. In the purple moon I go.

I am the purple moon; the purple moon is me.

We are now a BIG PURPLE WE!!

IN THE PURPLE MOON I GO!

In the purple land, here I am, what a grand and enchanting land. There are lilacs as far as I can see their sweet aroma consumes me. This place I came to be, makes me feel completely carefree. The lilacs project pure love from thee. Here in this GRAND PURPLE LAND, is where my spirit will grow, this I surely know.

TO THE LEFT THERE WAS A WARM GLOW!

TO THE LEFT THERE WAS A WARM GLOW!

TO THE RIGHT A LIGHT SO VERY BRIGHT!

TO THE RIGHT A LIGHT SO VERY BRIGHT!

we are the children of the light!

The warm glow to the left comes upon me, an echo of voices speaks in harmony. "We are the children of the light, and we welcome you this very night.

He takes me on a journey of happiness I did not know exist. He consumes me with complete bliss. He shows me a leaf blowing on a crisp fall day.

I am a leaf; the leaf is me.
I did not know that a leaf feels this free!

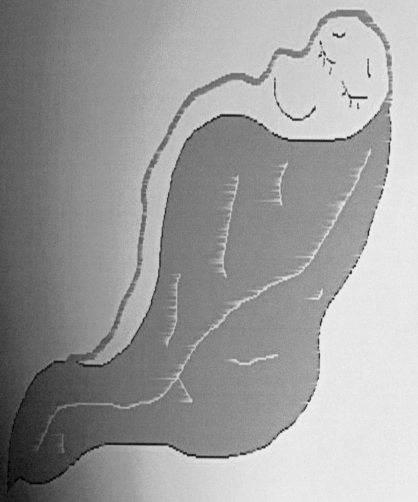

I became the leaf!

He shows me children laughing as they swirl around and around, their feet never touching the ground, their carefree little laughter so full of joy and glee. Delight gave me happiness in pure simplicity. Delight went away, I am thankful he showed me this happy day!

THEY SPIN AND SPIN!

I feel a soothing feeling of pure peace surrounding me. A soft delicate voice begins to speak. "I am peace you know me; I live within thee" I feel softness and a gentle touch and no touch as gentle as such. I smell roses, the roses become me. I lay on a cloud, the cloud as soft as a baby's touch. I am the cloud; the cloud is me. I feel such tranquility.

Peace is a wonderful place to be, peace has truly become me.

PEACE CAME TO ME FULL OF LOVE AND TRANQUILITY!

DARK DAY !

As I lay here in peace, I feel its presence slip away. All of a sudden, I'm in my darkest day.

The rain begins to fall, the land begins to flood. Higher and higher the water becomes; I am surrounded by the flood. This feeling is so scary and empty to me. I beg to be released from this Horrible Misery!!! The rain drops become heavier, I feel pain and sadness, I feel alone. My heart becomes hopeless. How could this misery consume me? The water begins to cover me entirely.

HOPE!

A light begins to shine so bright above me, on this dark and awful day. The light smiles and surrounds me. As the water becomes higher, I no longer feel any fear, because the light of hope is near. "Hold on my dear" the light calls out to me, "hold on to hope because I am always near." I feel a smile within in my heart.

The light of hope showed me this very dark day, Hope is always on its way! Up I come out of the water that surrounds me, because of Hope I believe in me, and this belief set my spirit free.

The bright light to the right!

There I was again in this glorious purple moon, back again with the children of the light, Peace, Hope and Delight. I turn to my right the light so very, very bright called out to me, but it isn't a voice, no not a voice you would think a voice to be. This voice is completely free, yes indeed!!

This bright light to the right is the brightest of bright!

PEACE

LOVE

HOPE

This light held me this very night, it gave me love, peace, hope and so much delight. The voice that you would not imagine the way a voice to be, told me the purple moon was where I should be. The purple moon the very bright light said to me, is the house for the children of the light, here my dear everything will always be alright. You now have the key to always set your spirit free, you are now "WE".

DELIGHT

WE!

LOVE

I feel my spirit illuminated with this extraordinary light. In the purple moon, I found my light this wonderful night.

The end

About the Author

Utterly devoted to inspiring and helping others, **Deidre Dorsett** is well-respected and widely appreciated light worker in the true sense of the word. What makes Deidre unique is her gift; she didn't learn how to spread light, she was born with this exceptional talent.

Even when she was at a very young age, Deidre has experienced outer body experiences. Having made contact with spiritual beings. She is a firm believer that there's a divine light of energy that is pure love, and concludes from her mind's eye,we are spirits experiencing a human experience. Her core mission is to spread that divine light.

Back in 1997, Deidre got an advertising design degree from the Art Institute of Atlanta. Ever since, she has been a freelance graphic designer with magical hands. It wasn't long until her talent got recognized. Today, she's the proud owner of her own brand known as Aringa Creations.

A courageous survivor that refuses to give up regardless of what life throws at her, Deidre has looked death in the eyes and loudly said – not this time! Although she has seen many dark days, Deidre remains a believer in the higher divinity.

Through her heart-touching, inspirational book The Purple Moon, Deidre hopes to reach more people and make them aware of their own spirituality. Within the pages of this book, readers find hope that brighter days are ahead. Thanks to Deidre's warm and accepting writing tone, The Purple Moon has the power to soothe one's soul.

Deidre Dorsett is a beloved mother of two and grandmother of four.

Printed in the United States
by Baker & Taylor Publisher Services